Barbie™ AND THE MAGIC of PEGASUS

A Junior Novelization

Adapted by Kari James

Based on the original screenplay by
Cliff Ruby & Elana Lesser

SCHOLASTIC INC.

New York   Toronto   London   Auckland   Sydney
Mexico City   New Delhi   Hong Kong   Buenos Aires

ISBN 0-439-78542-1

Special thanks to Vicki Jaeger, Monica Lopez, Rob Hudnut,
Shelley Dvi-Vardhana, Jesyca C. Durchin, Luke Carroll, Kelly Shin, Anita Lee,
Sean Newton, Mike Douglas, Dave Gagnon, Derek Goodfellow,
Teresa Johnston, and Walter P. Martishius.

Cover Design by Pamela Darcy
Interior Design by Bethany Dixon

Published by Scholastic Inc.
SCHOLASTIC and associated logos are trademarks
and/or registered trademarks of Scholastic Inc.

12 11 10 9 8 7 6 5 4 3 2 1   5 6 7 8 9/0

Printed in the U.S.A.
First printing, September 2005

Introduction

Long, long ago, high in the snowy mountains, a large flag decorated with a picture of a winged horse fluttered atop a beautiful walled castle. Inside the castle, the king and queen gazed happily at their newborn daughter sleeping peacefully in her bassinet.

"We'll keep her close to us," said the king.

"Safe from all evil," agreed his queen.

For many years, peace reigned in the mountain kingdom, and the king and queen lived with their daughter in blissful safety.

But on the princess's seventeenth birthday, everything changed for the royal family . . . as it had once in the past, years before the princess had been born. . . .

Chapter 1
Annika's Adventure

Whoosh! Princess Annika's blond hair blew out behind her as she skated down a frozen river. All she could hear was the sound of her skates cutting into the ice. She bent low to gain speed — then leaped into the air over a log. It felt like flying! Down the mountain she zoomed, skating and jumping, until —

Whoa! The princess leaned too far forward and lost her balance. Down she tumbled until

she slid out onto a frozen pond —

Oh, no! What was that furry thing up ahead?

Crash! Annika hurtled into a cold snowdrift. Chuckling to herself, she sat up and brushed the snow out of her eyes.

Shivering in front of her was an adorable white bear cub.

"Uh-oh," said the bear in a cute little growling voice.

"Don't be afraid," Annika told her. Then the princess noticed how badly the bear was shivering. "Why, you're cold! I've never seen a cold polar bear before. Don't you have a family?"

The bear cub shook her head sadly.

Annika gently picked up the little bear and hugged her close. "Now you do," she whispered. "My name's Annika, and I think I'll call you Shiver. Come on, let's go home."

Annika managed to slip back into the castle without being seen by the guards. She was sneaking up the stairs to her room when her parents, the king and queen, rushed toward her.

"Annika! You're safe!" they cried. "Where have you been? We've been looking everywhere for you!"

"I was just skating," said Annika, hiding Shiver behind her.

"How many times have we told you? Don't ever leave the castle without our permission!" her parents insisted.

Shiver popped her head around Annika to see what all the fuss was about.

"A bear?" gasped the queen.

Shiver looked sweetly at the queen, and the queen relaxed a little.

"She has such a sweet little face," the queen said, "but she could bite or scratch you, Annika!"

"This is what comes from leaving the castle," the king said sternly. "Annika, your mother and I can't take this constant worrying. No more ice-skating. It's for your own good."

"Father, Mother, please!" cried Annika. "I love skating. Please don't do this!"

"Your skates, please," said the king, holding out his hand.

Annika hung her head as she gave up her beloved skates.

"You don't understand anything," she sobbed, running up the stairs. "It's not fair! I hate you!"

The king and queen looked at each other and sighed sadly. Annika didn't know that protecting her was as difficult for them as it was for her.

Chapter 2
Wenlock

As the moon rose over the castle that evening, Annika sat slumped on her bed while beside her Shiver played with the princess's jewels.

"How could my parents do this to me — especially on my seventeenth birthday?" cried Annika. With a sad sigh, she went out on her balcony to watch the falling snow. She could hear lively music playing beyond the castle walls. A party was going on nearby — at the frozen pond!

Annika made a quick decision. Putting a finger to her lips, she gestured for Shiver to remain quiet.

The little bear nodded in understanding.

"Come on now, Shiver," whispered Annika. "Let's go to a party!"

It didn't take long for Annika to find where her father had put her ice skates. Then she snuck out of the palace and hurried to the village pond. Soon she was happily gliding and twirling with the friendly villagers. It was the best birthday of her life!

The fun didn't last long. A harsh wind blew through the trees. What was that cold light shooting across the sky? Everyone backed away as they saw a dark, winged creature flying toward them — with a mean-looking man riding on its back! The man held a magic wand that glowed with an eerie blue light.

The man and the scary creature — a griffin, with the head of an eagle and the body of a lion — landed right in front of Annika. She tried not to cower in fear as he blocked her from escaping.

"Allow me to introduce myself," said the man, bowing to Annika with a wicked smile. "I'm Wenlock — your future husband." He pulled a big, gaudy ring out of his pocket. "I'm offering you the once-in-a-lifetime opportunity to be my bride."

Annika was so frightened, she could hardly breathe. "Your *bride?*" she gasped.

At that moment, the king and queen rode up in their carriage, surrounded by their royal guards. They had seen the strange blue light in the sky and knew that the evil wizard Wenlock was near. When they'd discovered that Annika was missing, they knew she must be at the village party.

"Let her be, Wenlock," ordered the king.

"Please spare her!" cried the queen.

Wenlock sneered. "Are you telling me what to do?" he asked. "Maybe you have forgotten what happened to your *other* daughter."

Annika shook her head in confusion. "What other daughter?" she asked her parents.

Neither the king nor the queen answered Annika's question. "Go, Wenlock," the king insisted instead. "You already have a wife."

"I *did*. Three wives, in fact," Wenlock said. "Now Annika's the lucky girl. Marry me!"

"No!" cried Annika.

Wenlock became furious. Raising his wand, he fired a spell at the king and queen. "Petrify them!" he shouted.

A flash encircled Annika's parents. Instantly

they turned into marble statues! As Annika screamed, Wenlock raised his wand again and made the entire village and all the people in it as hard and cold as stone. A creepy silence hung in the frigid air.

"You're next," Wenlock told Annika, "unless you marry me."

"B-but —" stammered Annika, feeling despair. What could she do now? She was trapped in the wizard's evil plan.

That's when a beautiful flying horse wearing a crown soared down from the sky. The gorgeous creature avoided the griffin and landed between Annika and Wenlock. "Grab on!" the horse told Annika.

Desperate to escape Wenlock, Annika grabbed on to the horse's neck while Shiver clutched Annika's feet. Away they flew, faster than the wind.

Wenlock watched angrily from below, surrounded by the frozen townspeople. "Three days!" he thundered. "You have three days to marry me, or these people stay like this . . . *forever.*"

Chapter 3
In the Palace of the Cloud Queen

As the winged horse flew higher into the sky, Annika cried, "I have to go back. I have to stop him!"

The horse shook her head. "You can't," she said. "Nobody can stop Wenlock — not as long as he has that wand he stole from a powerful sorcerer. I can't let him hurt you."

"Who are you?" Annika asked.

"A friend," said the horse mysteriously. She said no more, until she approached a palace made of clouds that reached high into the sky.

Annika and Shiver had never seen anything so beautiful.

"Where are we?" asked Annika breathlessly.

"Cloud Kingdom," replied the horse, soaring toward the castle.

Annika could see three little girls waving at them from the veranda of the palace. Each girl had her own flying pony!

The flying horse swooped right through the palace gates, flying inside where everything was made of gleaming crystal. The hallways and staircases seemed to go on forever. Most amazing of all were the flying horses everywhere, with their long, flowing manes and glittering wings.

The horse flew on until she reached a hall where a lovely woman sat on a throne. After landing in front of the woman, the horse bowed deeply and said, "Your Highness."

The queen smiled at the winged horse.

"Brietta, you've brought visitors. What has happened?"

"Wenlock," replied Brietta. "Annika, this is Rayla, the Cloud Queen."

Annika and Shiver bowed their heads in front of the beautiful queen. "Pleased to meet you, Your Majesty," said Annika.

"What did Wenlock do this time?" asked Queen Rayla.

With a shudder, Annika replied, "Wenlock turned my parents — and everyone else — into marble! If I don't agree to marry him in three days, he'll never turn them back to the way they were."

The queen sighed. "I'm so sorry," she said. "Come rest now." She led Annika, Shiver, and Brietta to a large, shimmering bedroom, where the three little Cloud Princesses — Blush, Rose, and Lilac — gave Annika a warm dress to wear and brushed her hair. They brushed Brietta's mane, too, and gave Shiver a cozy bed to snuggle into.

"We've never had a real person here before, except for your sister, of course," Princess Blush told Annika.

"My sister?" asked Annika, surprised.

"Why, Brietta is your sister!" said Blush.

"B-but . . . she's a —" stuttered Annika.

"A Pegasus — a flying horse," said Blush. "But she used to be just like you."

Annika turned to Brietta. "You're my — my sister?" she asked the horse.

"Yes," replied Brietta.

"But how? What happened?" asked Annika. She could hardly believe she had a sister and never knew it!

The horse closed her eyes. "It's too painful to talk about," she said sadly.

The Cloud Queen stroked Brietta's mane. "Wenlock cast a spell on her," she told Annika. "It was her seventeenth birthday — and just like you, she refused to marry him. So he gave her wings and a tail. Your parents did all they could to break the spell, but nothing worked. Brietta couldn't bear to see them unhappy, so she left . . . and found refuge with us here in Cloud Kingdom."

"Why didn't my parents tell me this?" cried Annika.

"I guess they didn't know how to," replied Brietta. "They kept it a secret and moved to the farthest corner of the kingdom. There they built a new castle, making it as safe as they could. They were so afraid Wenlock would come after you! And he did. . . ."

Annika hung her head. "I never knew why they worried so much about me. I . . . I have to save them and tell them I'm sorry I was so angry with them." She looked up at the Cloud

Queen. "Can you help me, Your Highness?"

The Cloud Queen shook her head sadly. "I have no power over Wenlock."

"There has to be something I can do," insisted Annika.

"What about the Wand of Light?" asked Princess Rose.

"What's the Wand of Light?" asked Annika.

"It's nothing," said Brietta. "Just a myth. They say it has the most powerful magic — even more powerful than Wenlock's. You make it from a Measure of Courage, a Gem of Ice lit by Hope's Eternal Flame, and a Ring of Love."

"We can do that!" cried Annika.

"It doesn't exist," said Brietta bitterly. "I've tried for years . . . it's hopeless."

A large bell pealed and Blush, Rose, and

Lilac jumped up. It was time for them to fly into the morning sky on their winged ponies and paint the colors of the sunrise. Each princess had the same color paint as her name.

Annika watched the young princesses welcome the dawn. She could feel the morning light giving her strength and hope. "I'm going to build the Wand of Light," she announced.

After some convincing, Brietta agreed to

take Annika to the deepest, darkest part of the Forbidden Forest.

The Cloud Queen hung a delicate crystal bell around Brietta's neck to ring if she ever needed her.

Annika picked up Shiver and climbed onto Brietta's back. They flew out of the Cloud Palace, beginning a journey they would never forget.

Chapter 4
In the Forbidden Forest

"Brietta, what's the Forbidden Forest like?" asked Annika as they flew high up over snowy fields toward the edge of the woods.

"Dark and scary," warned Brietta.

"It sounds like the perfect place to find a Measure of Courage," said Annika hopefully.

Once they entered the gloomy forest, Shiver got spooked, fell into an ice gully, and slid out of sight. When Annika and Brietta tried to go after her, they both got caught in snare traps that pulled them off their feet and left them dangling from tree branches.

Luckily, a handsome blacksmith named Aidan heard the sisters' struggle and cut them

out of the traps with a sword he had made himself. He warned them to get out of the area quickly — the giant who had set the traps lived nearby!

Annika had to find Shiver before the giant did! As soon as she was free, she jumped in the ice gully and slid after the little polar bear, zooming at top speed.

When Annika flew out the end of the gully, she found Shiver — but she also found that they were now in the huge cooking pot of a giant named Ollie! It wouldn't be long until she and Shiver would be soup.

Annika had to think fast. Realizing the giant wasn't all that smart, Annika said, "Poor Ollie. Compared to the giant down the road, you're just a weakling."

"Ollie strong! Ollie can do anything!" shouted the outraged giant.

"Well, the other giant can tie himself to a post with a huge chain, lock it up, then break free with a single breath," said Annika.

Ollie lashed the chain around himself and locked it to a post . . . but then he couldn't break the chain!

Annika quickly tied her long hair ribbon to a piece of carrot that was in the pot and tossed it up. It lodged itself around the pot handle. With Shiver on her back, she climbed up the ribbon. They were free!

On the way back into the forest, they ran into Brietta and Aidan.

"I was going to rescue you *again,* but you beat me to it," said Aidan. His eyes shined with admiration.

Annika proudly held up her hair ribbon and told how she'd escaped.

"Annika, hold it higher," said Brietta. "Look! It's your exact height! Your exact measure . . . a Measure of Courage."

The ribbon sparkled. Then it stiffened and turned into a glowing silver rod!

"A staff," whispered Annika in awe, "for the Wand of Light."

"Now we need 'a Gem of Ice lit by Hope's Eternal Flame,'" said Brietta.

Aidan snickered. "It doesn't exist," he said, rolling his eyes. He turned to go home.

Before he could disappear into the forest, Annika noticed Aidan's elaborate sword.

"Wait," she said. "When we have the three

parts of the wand, we'll need somebody with your sword-making skills to put them together. Please help me — I only have three days to save my parents."

Aidan turned serious. "Okay," he agreed.

Chapter 5
Hope's Eternal Flame

Aidan knew a man named Ferris who sold stolen goods — that seemed as good a place as any to start looking for the gem. After walking all night, the group reached Ferris's riverside shack.

Unfortunately, Ferris didn't have what they were looking for, but luckily he had heard about "a Gem of Ice lit by Hope's Eternal Flame."

Gallantly, Aidan offered to sell his beautiful sword for Ferris's information, but Annika stopped him and traded her jeweled ice skates instead.

Ferris told them that he had a map that might lead to a buried treasure chest that held the gem. The map had been brought in by a man who'd claimed to have the gem.

Unfortunately, after the man brought in the map, he was never seen again.

"Because of Wenlock?" asked Aidan.

"Yes," said Ferris. "Here, take the map. I don't want anything to do with it."

The friends set off to find the gem with Ferris's map.

After a day of searching in the cold — and getting lost — they suspected that Ferris had lied and the map was a fake! The friends had to spend that night in a cold cave.

They didn't feel warm again until the first rays of the sun finally arrived the next morning. "It's our last day," sighed Annika, looking up at the sky.

"Our last hope," added Brietta.

Annika's face brightened. "That's it!" she

cried. "What says hope more than the dawn? The sunrise is Hope's Eternal Flame!"

As the friends watched the sunshine light up an ice-blue glacier, Annika said, "See how the sun shines on the glacier? It looks like a gem of ice! The gem's somewhere on top of that glacier — I can feel it."

In a flash, Annika, Aidan, and Shiver jumped onto Brietta's back to fly to the top of the glacier. There wasn't a moment to lose!

Little did they know that Ferris had warned Wenlock that Annika was near, and at that very moment the griffin was searching for her.

Chapter 6
A Ring of Love

Brietta landed on the glacier, and Annika smiled when she spied some stepping-stones that led down into a hollow in the snow. With Aidan right behind her, she followed the steps, which led to an icy wall. Wiping away the snow, the princess was thrilled to find what looked like a door with ancient writing carved into the ice. It had to be a clue! But what did it say?

Aidan was able to read the mysterious runes. *"Beware: Take only what you need, but never from greed,"* he read aloud.

As Aidan finished reading, the ice sparkled and the ground rumbled . . . the ice fell away . . . and a secret passageway appeared, leading into a huge cave! Far ahead in the cave's darkness, a light glowed. Shiver sniffed the air,

then bounded ahead toward the light. After hiking a bit, the friends were amazed to find that Shiver had led them to a chamber full of hundreds of glittering diamonds!

"'Parkle!" cried Shiver happily.

"These are star diamonds!" exclaimed Brietta.

Annika's eyes fell on a beautiful diamond set off on its own, flashing in the sun. "A Gem of Ice lit by Hope's Eternal Flame," she whispered. With a heart full of hope, she reached for the gem. She remembered what the runes had said: *Take what you need, never from greed* . . . so she took only the one diamond. Aidan took a medium-size star diamond, too.

The cavern rumbled . . . but then became quiet again.

Little Shiver hadn't understood the ancient warning. She squealed, grabbing dozens of diamonds.

BOOM! The cavern started to shake.

"Shiver, no!" cried Annika, pulling the bear cub away from the diamonds. As heavy chunks of ice fell from the ceiling, the friends knew they had only seconds to fly out of the ice cavern and escape the coming avalanche!

Brietta burst through the opening of the cave as the glacier began to crack. Moments later, the mountain of ice collapsed with a roar — sealing off the cavern of diamonds forever.

As Brietta flew her friends into the sky, Annika held the staff near the diamond she had retrieved from the cave. A magical burst of energy surrounded Annika, and then the diamond began to glow!

"Now all we need is the Ring of Love," cried Annika happily. "Then I can break Wenlock's spell!"

"Maybe I could forge a ring," offered Aidan.

Brietta landed so Aidan could build a fire.

Aidan was about to put his precious sword

into the flames to make the ring when Brietta stepped forward and let Annika take her glittering crown. "For our parents," she said. "I want to do it. I love them."

The crown began to glow in Annika's hands! "The Ring of Love," she said in wonder. "That's right! No one said the ring had to be for your finger."

Aidan wasted no time in heating Brietta's crown in the flames so that he could hammer it onto the sparkling staff. Then all he had to do was press the star diamond into the warm metal of the crown.

The Wand of Light was finally ready.

Chapter 7
The Wand of Light

"Will it work?" asked Aidan as the friends stared at the wand.

"How will we know?" asked Brietta.

Annika held the wand near the flying horse. Closing her eyes, she said, "Wand of Light, I wish from the bottom of my heart to break Wenlock's spell over my sister."

A blaze of light flared around the wand. It glowed . . . the diamond sparkled . . . magical dust whirled around Brietta and lifted her off the ground! With a flash of light and a gust of wind, Brietta transformed into the girl she had been before — a beautiful young princess of seventeen!

"You're back," breathed Annika.

Brietta reached out to hug her sister. "Thank you — thank you so much!" she cried.

"We *can* beat Wenlock!" cried Annika. "Come on, let's go home."

That's when Brietta rang the magical bell the Cloud Queen had given her. Soon, out of the night sky flew two graceful horses with wings. After saying good-bye to Aidan, the sisters and Shiver flew off on horseback to save their parents.

They did not know that Wenlock's griffin had been watching. With an angry squawk, the griffin soared away to tell the evil wizard what he'd seen.

It didn't take long for Wenlock to catch up to the princesses. With his wand, he zapped Brietta off her winged horse. Brietta plummeted toward the ground.

On her own steed, Annika swooped down and caught her sister. She'd flown too low, though, and they all crashed into the snow. Annika quickly sprang to her feet, but Brietta lay in the snow, badly hurt.

Wenlock circled around them and landed nearby.

"You hurt her!" Annika shouted. "How dare you!" She aimed the Wand of Light at the wizard and screamed, "Destroy Wenlock!"

But since it was used in anger, the wand didn't work!

"Did you really think you could beat me?" Wenlock asked.

"Okay, okay," said Annika, feeling confused

and defeated. "Release my parents and the others . . . and I'll . . . I'll marry you."

"You think I still want *you?*" asked Wenlock. "After you just tried to destroy me?" With a laugh, he covered Annika with so much snow that she couldn't move. Then he grabbed the

Wand of Light, hopped onto the griffin's back, and flew away.

As soon as Wenlock was gone, Shiver woke up Brietta. The two of them frantically tried to dig Annika out of her snowy prison.

That's when Aidan rode up to help. He'd decided to stay close behind the princesses and watch over them. He dug Annika out of the snow, but she would not wake up. "I never should have left you," he whispered.

The friends climbed onto the winged horses and quickly flew off to the Cloud Kingdom to try to save Annika.

When Annika finally woke up, Aidan was right by her side.

"It's almost sundown," said Annika, even though she was feeling weak. "I need to get the

Wand of Light before sunset!"

"But it's with Wenlock," said Brietta. "His palace is surrounded by sheer ice. There's no way in. And it didn't work against him before, remember?"

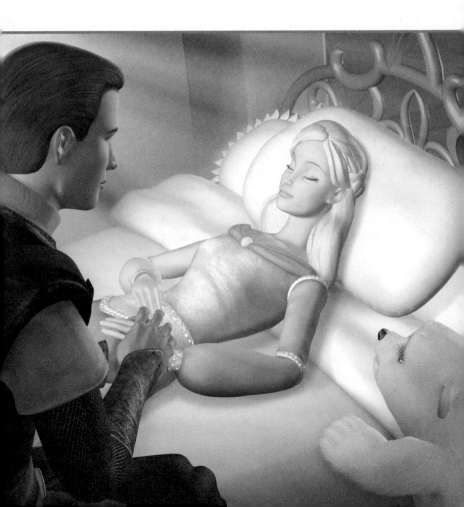

Annika smiled mysteriously. "We'll see," she said. Annika was determined to leave the palace and face the evil wizard one last time, so the Cloud Queen did all she could do to help. She told the three Cloud Princesses to paint the bright colors of the sunset as usual, but to do it as slowly as possible to give Annika more time to beat Wenlock's evil spell. Then she surrounded the friends with a cloud so the griffin wouldn't see them flying to the wizard's palace.

They were ready to try again.

Chapter 8
The Battle for the Wand

While Brietta waited outside with the winged horses, Aidan, Shiver, and Annika skated down an icy tunnel that led to Wenlock's home.

Inside, Wenlock was up to no good. He was in his throne room, playing with the Wand of Light. He raised the wand and pointed it at the sad troll women who worked for him day and night. "Wand of Light, make these trolls work

double time," he commanded. But the wand didn't work. Wenlock angrily tossed it into a chest with other treasures with which he'd grown bored. He threw it so hard that the star diamond nearly came loose.

Meanwhile, the friends had sneaked into the castle — and the griffin spotted them!

Now it was up to Aidan to battle the griffin with his sword while Annika and Shiver tried to find the wand. The sun was setting — only a few minutes were left!

Shiver could smell Wenlock's treasures. She led Annika into the throne room, and they quickly found the Wand of Light.

Wenlock had heard his griffin battling with Aidan and knew Annika must be in the castle, too. He searched the throne room, but luckily she and Shiver had managed to hide behind the big chest that held the Wand of Light. When Wenlock left to search another room, Annika pulled the wand out of the chest. The star diamond broke off of the wand and slid across the slippery floor . . . out the window . . . and off a balcony!

At that moment, Aidan appeared. He'd managed to escape the griffin and crawl up to the balcony to Annika.

"Aidan! The diamond's gone!" cried Annika.

Aidan reached into his pocket and pulled out the star diamond he'd taken for himself. "How about this one?" he asked, setting the diamond in place.

That's when Wenlock found them. He used

his evil magic to knock the wand from Annika's hand!

"Get the wand!" Wenlock ordered his trolls. Aidan charged at Wenlock, but the griffin appeared and pinned Aidan down with one huge claw. One of the trolls grabbed the wand.

Meanwhile, up in the sky, the Cloud Princesses looked anxiously at the sunset. "That's it," said Rose sadly. "We can't slow the sunset any more."

Blush hung her head and said, "Wenlock's spell will last forever."

Chapter 9
Magic in the Air

Annika noticed that all the trolls were wearing what looked like wedding rings — and she realized something important about the trolls!

"You must've been terrible to your wives," Annika told Wenlock. "If I had the Wand of Light, I'd make life better for *everyone*." She watched the trolls' faces to see what they thought of that.

Wenlock held out his hand to one of the trolls. "Give me the Wand of Light," he ordered.

The troll waited and looked at Annika.

"I believe the Wand of Light will save us all," Annika told the trolls.

"Give it to me!" Wenlock shouted at the troll.

The troll looked at her friends. She threw the Wand of Light . . . to Annika!

Annika pointed the wand at Wenlock. "For the love of my family and my people, I ask you to break all of Wenlock's spells," she said.

Wenlock pointed his own wand at Annika, but the Wand of Light's good magic was more powerful than Wenlock's bad magic. A burst of good magic lifted Annika into the air and gave

her special powers. Her torn dress turned into a beautiful gown, her shoes became delicate lavender slippers, and a glittering crown appeared on her head.

"No!" cried Wenlock. He knew he had been beaten. The magic from Annika's wand melted Wenlock's wand into nothingness.

Then the Wand of Light changed everything for everyone.

The scary griffin turned back into its true self — a scrawny cat.

The troll women became beautiful women once again, as they looked when Wenlock had married them.

Best of all, far away at the village pond, the marble that held Annika's parents shattered. The king and queen — along with all the villagers — were human once more!

And Wenlock? He was no longer a powerful wizard. He'd turned back into *his* old self — a small, silly-looking man, wearing clothes that were much too big for him!

"How'd you do this?" Wenlock screeched at Annika. "The wand was useless."

"I learned the hard way that the Wand of Light doesn't work when it's used in anger," Annika replied.

The palace began to shake. Parts of the ceiling crumbled to the floor. Any moment now, the palace would tumble to pieces!

Brietta appeared with the flying horses, ready to take Annika, Aidan, and Shiver home.

"Hurry!" Annika told Wenlock's wives. "You're free now. Go!"

"Thank you for your help," said one of the wives.

"But we have a little unfinished business," said another wife.

They all stepped toward Wenlock.

"Now, now, let's talk about this," said Wenlock nervously as his wives, who were now much taller than he, came closer. "We were married once, remember?"

As the friends flew away safely, they saw Wenlock's castle break off the mountain — and crash into the sea.

Wenlock and his wives managed to survive the collapse and ended up together in the water, floating on a large chunk of ice.

Looking up to where his palace had stood, Wenlock cried, "Everything's gone — gone!"

"Not us, Wenlock, not us!" one wife said with a laugh. She handed him an oar. "Now paddle — and when we get to our new home, let's see how you like cleaning floors."

One of the other wives giggled. "How did you used to put it, Wenlock? Oh, yes. 'Work double time.'"

Chapter 10
Reunion

When she got back to her parents' castle, Annika rushed happily into her mother's and father's arms.

"You're home!" cried the queen happily. "Not a scratch? Not a bump?"

"What about Wenlock?" asked the king anxiously.

Annika smiled. "He won't be bothering us anymore. Now, are you ready for a surprise?"

Smiling shyly, Brietta appeared at the door.

"Brietta? Is that really you?" gasped the queen.

"Mother! Father!" cried Brietta, as her parents ran toward her and enveloped her in a warm embrace. It had been so long.

"This is impossible!" cried the king happily.

"It was Annika," said Brietta. "She never gave up hope!"

The queen turned to Annika. "We owe you so much," she said.

"No, I owe you . . . an apology," said Annika, looking at her parents. "I said such terrible things and I snuck out of the palace. I know now that you were just trying to protect me from Wenlock."

"We should've told you the truth long ago," admitted the king.

"Shall we call it even?" asked Annika, hugging her father again.

It was good to be home.

Chapter 11
A Happy Ending

A few days later, Annika, Shiver, Brietta, and Aidan went back to the Cloud Castle to thank the Cloud Queen for her wonderful help in saving the kingdom.

Annika and Aidan had quickly realized that they didn't want to be apart. With all the danger behind them, they were now free to have fun together.

As everyone happily watched the couple

skate together on a magical cloud, Brietta handed the Wand of Light to the Cloud Queen. "Will you keep this safe, Your Highness?" she asked.

The queen nodded. "I'd be honored," she replied. "It will be the first star in the sky every night . . . and a reflection of the love between Annika and Aidan."

The three Cloud Princesses toddled onto the ice with Annika and Aidan. "Whoa!" they cried, trying not to fall.

Shiver didn't want to miss out on all the fun, and it wasn't long before she was slipping and sliding on the ice . . . and crashing into everyone!

"Gotta love her," said Annika with a giggle as she skated hand in hand with Aidan.

"Yeah," said Aidan, looking tenderly at Annika. He led her into a twirl. As Annika leaped into the air, he caught her. They were together in a world all their own, and Aidan knew he'd never let her go again.

See *Barbie*™ in Her First Ever *Fairytopia*™ Movie!

Now on **DVD** VIDEO & Video